This item was purchased with funds donated by:

A. Sturm & Sons Foundation, Inc.

The Paperboy

story and paintings by
Dav Pilkey

Orchard Books   New York

Orchard Books, A Grolier Company, 95 Madison Avenue, New York, NY 10016

Manufactured in the United States of America. Printed and bound by
Phoenix Color Corp. The text of this book is set in 24 point Times New Roman. The illustrations are acrylics and india ink reproduced in full color.

Hardcover 10 9 8 7 6 5 4   Paperback 10 9 8 7 6 5 4 3

Library of Congress Cataloging-in-Publication Data. Pilkey, Dav, date. The paperboy / story and paintings by Dav Pilkey.
p.   cm. "A Richard Jackson book"—Half t.p. Summary: A paperboy and his dog enjoy the quiet of the early morning as they go about their rounds. ISBN 0-531-09506-1 (tr.) ISBN 0-531-08856-1 (lib. bdg.) ISBN 0-531-07139-1 (pbk.)
[1. Newspaper carriers—Fiction. 2. Morning—Fiction.] I. Title. PZ7.P63123Pap 1996 95-30641

MORNING
STAR
GAZETTE

With thanks to Kinney Whitmore

The mornings of the paperboy
are still dark
and they are always cold
even in the summer.

And on these cold mornings
the paperboy's bed is still warm
and it is always hard to get out—
even for his dog . . .

. . . but they do.

And softly they step down
the quiet hall
past the door where the paperboy's
father and mother are sleeping.

Past the door where his sister
is asleep.

And down to the kitchen
where they eat from their bowls.

And out to the garage
where they quickly fold their papers,
snapping on green rubber bands
and placing them in a large red bag.

It's hard to ride a bike
when you are loaded down with newspapers.
But the paperboy has learned how to do this,
and he is good at it.

The paperboy knows his route by heart,
so he doesn't ever think about
which house to pedal to.

Instead, he is thinking about other things.
Big Things.
And small things.
And sometimes he is thinking about
nothing at all.

His dog, too, knows this route by heart.
He knows which trees are for sniffing.
He knows which birdbaths are for drinking,
which squirrels are for chasing, and
which cats are for growling at.

All the world is asleep
except for the paperboy
and his dog.
And this is the time
when they are the happiest.

But little by little
the world around them wakes up.

The stars and the moon fade away
and the skies become orange and pink.

And when the paperboy has delivered
his last newspaper,
he and his dog race home.

And his empty red bag flaps behind him
in the cold morning air.

Soon they are back home.
It is still dark inside,
but the sounds of morning are all around.
His father and mother are awake
and talking softly in their bed,

and his sister is downstairs watching
Saturday morning cartoons.

And back inside his own room
the paperboy pulls down his shade
and crawls back into his bed,
which is still warm.

And while all of the world is waking up,
the paperboy is going back to sleep
and his dog is sleeping, too.
Their work is done . . .

...and now is the time for dreaming.

Fans Love Reading
Choose Your Own Adventure®!

"The demand for these books never really abated and you have made this children's librarian's dream come true."

**Marge Loch-Wouters,
Menasha Public Library, Menasha WI**

"We have had these books in our library ever since their first publishing. They have never gone out of demand."

**Jean Closz, Blount County
Public Library, Maryville TN**

"*Choose Your Own Adventure* taught me to choose carefully since every decision has consequences. One day, I hope to teach as a professor of literature and instill an enthusiasm for reading in others."

Jeff Greenwell, UC Riverside

Watch for these titles coming up in the

CHOOSE YOUR OWN ADVENTURE®

Dragonlarks™ series

Ask your bookseller for books you have missed
or visit us at cyoa.com to learn more.

YOUR VERY OWN ROBOT
by R. A. Montgomery
INDIAN TRAIL
by R. A. Montgomery
CARAVAN
by R. A. Montgomery
THE HAUNTED HOUSE
by R. A. Montgomery
YOUR PURRR-FECT BIRTHDAY
by R. A. Montgomery
GHOST ISLAND
by Shannon Gilligan
SAND CASTLE
by R. A. Montgomery

MORE TITLES COMING SOON!

www.cyoa.com

THE LAKE MONSTER MYSTERY

BY SHANNON GILLIGAN

A DRAGONLARK BOOK

You and your older sister Hannah are at your grandparents' summer house on Lake Champlain in Vermont. You visit the lake every summer, but this year is special. You have decided to spend your visit searching for Champ, a sea creature who lives in the lake.

Many people have spotted Champ over the years. They say that Champ has a big head covered in scales, a slender neck, and a long, snakelike body. Champ has never attacked anyone. Scientists believe that Champ is very gentle and shy. In fact, Champ is so shy that no one has ever gotten a photograph of her. Maybe you and Hannah will be the first!

Turn the next page.

It is a warm sunny day with only a few clouds in the sky—a perfect day to begin. You put on your life jackets, grab the camera, and head for the canoe. As you look across the lack, you realize that searching for Champ is going to be a big job!

"Where do you want to go first?" Hannah asks. "We could go to Shelburne Point, where some people saw Champ last summer, or we could head up toward Grande Isle.

"Grand Isle might be better because there are lots of quiet, deep coves there. Remember, Champ is very shy."

If you decide to go to Shelburne Point, turn to page 4.

If you decide to head toward Grande Isle, turn to page 7.

You paddle your canoe toward Shelburne Point. In 15 minutes you can see the famous house on the point.

"Let's drift for a while," Hannah suggests. "It might be a good time to try out your bait."

"Good idea." You reach for a wire basket tied to a fishing line. Inside the wire basket are some large, fresh shrimp. Last year some picnickers saw Champ in a spot where they had dropped some shrimp salad out of their boat. You figure it's worth a try.

After gently letting the basket overboard, you lean back and close your eyes. The sun beats down on your bare arms. Hannah hums quietly to herself. Several minutes later you feel a quick tug at the fishing line. Jolting awake, you look overboard. The water is so dark you can't see anything. Then you feel a second tug—a stronger one.

If you pull the basket up right away, turn to page 18.

If you wait for another tug, turn to page 11.

You paddle home quickly and show the stones to your grandparents. Your grandmother is sure the stones are real emeralds, so you grandfather calls the police to make a report.

Two police off-icers come by later that after-noon. They look at the stones. Sure enough, they are emer-alds. The police officers tell you that they are

from an unsolved burglary from 70 years ago.

"Where did you get them?" one of the officers asks. Your grandparents point to you and Hannah.

"You've done a fine job," the officer says, smiling. "We gave up looking for these years ago. Have you two ever thought about detective work?"

"Not for now," you reply. "We have to keep looking for Champ."

The End

You and Hannah head the canoe toward Grand Isle. Out on the lake the waves are high. You arms begin to ache from paddling, but all you can think about is getting safely across the rough waters and finding Champ.

After 30 minutes of hard paddling you are close to Grand Isle. When you are 50 feet from shore you see an old abandoned house tucked beside a quiet cove. That's funny, you think. You've never noticed it before.

"Wow!" Hannah shouts. "It looks like a haunted house." As she speaks, a cloud passes in front of the sun.

Turn to the next page.

"Hey, Hannah!" you say. "Let's go in and explore the place."

"Okay. I'm getting tired anyway."

You continue paddling, and after a few minutes you pull the canoe up on the sandy shore.

As you walk toward the house, a chilly wind rises. You hear a long, eerie screech. An old shutter on the second story of the house breaks off. It tumbles through the air and lands right in front of you!

You and Hannah look at each other. "This place gives me the creeps," you say.

"It was just the wind," Hannah says. "The house isn't haunted. That's only in the movies."

If you decide it's safe to go inside, turn to page 10.

If you decide to leave, turn to page 17.

You shrug. Hannah is probably right. The two of you start off again toward the front door of the house.

The door opens when you shove it. You stumble into a dusty hallway.

"Hannah, it looks as if no one has been here for years!"

"I know," she says. "Let's give it a look."

Turn to page 14.

You decide to wait before bringing up the basket of shrimp. Champ scares easily. You don't want to frighten her off.

After a few minutes, there are no more tugs. You lean back against your cushion and doze.

Hannah's voice awakens you. "It looks like a storm. Don't you think we had better head in?"

"You're right. We can use the dock at Shelburne Point. That's closest."

As you paddle on, the rain starts to fall. Soon the lake is smooth from the steady pounding of the rain. It looks eerie and beautiful. The boats have all gone in to shelter, and you are alone on the lake.

Turn to the next page.

Before you move any farther, you hear splashing sounds about 20 feet from the shore. Looking up, you see not one but three sea creatures floating gracefully nearby. What great luck!

They look at you for a moment and then quickly dive back below the surface. You were so excited that you even forgot to take a picture!

Paddling home after the storm, you wonder if anyone will ever believe you.

The End

You tiptoe carefully from room to room. There are pieces of broken furniture, an old bird's nest, and lots of dust.

"There's nothing here. Let's go."

"Wait, Hannah. Look at this." You point to a narrow staircase behind a kitchen door. "This looks safe. Let's explore upstairs."

Hannah follows you up the dark, narrow staircase. It leads to a stuffy room. You carefully look through the closet and a chest of drawers. There's nothing else but a moth-eaten bed.

But wait! Hannah lifts up the mattress and finds a wooden box underneath.

Turn to page 16

16

She tries to open it, but the box is locked!

You wonder what's inside.

If you decide to take the box home and open it with your grandfather's tools, turn to page 30

If you decide to take the box home and open it with your grandfather's tools, turn to page 30

If you decide to open the box right now by breaking the lock with a rock, turn to page 34

"Hannah, let's not go in. That house looks dangerous. Why don't we build a sand castle instead?"

Hannah nods and the two of you choose a good spot and begin work. You lose track of time. A half hour passes before you notice the house is creaking in a strong wind. The skies are cloudy and dark. Thunder rumbles in the distance. A thunderstorm will start any minute.

You must do something—and fast!

If you decide to try to head for home in the canoe, turn to page 23.

If you run to the high rocks at the edge of the cove to signal for help, turn to page 33.

You yank the line and peer into the dark water. No luck
The basket comes up empty. Whatever it was, it wasn'
Champ.

Go on to the next page.

Hannah looks at the dripping basket and says, "It was probably just a fish. We'd better get going, anyway. There's a storm coming."

Turn to the next page.

Sure enough, the sky is filling with dark, heavy clouds.

You point your canoe toward home and paddle with all your strength. The wind howls and the lake gets choppy and rough.

"This is dangerous, Hannah. If the waves get any higher, we'll be swamped!"

"But we're almost home!" Hannah yells.

You peer ahead, but you still can't see the dock. Then you glance at the shore. It looks rocky, but it might be better to pull in and wait for the storm to end.

If you decide to continue home, turn to page 22.

If you tell Hannah that you think it's too dangerous to continue, and you want to wait on shore, turn to page 26.

Hannah is probably right. You decide to continue home. You get a firm grip on your slippery paddle and set to work.

In a minute the rain begins, first softly and then in a torrent. You keep paddling, but the lake is so rough that you aren't getting anywhere. The canoe drifts danger-ously close to shore.

Then there is a sudden crack—the loudest you have ever heard—and a flash of light. You are thrown from the

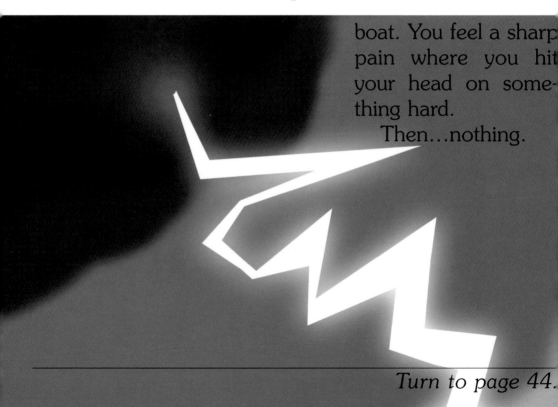

boat. You feel a sharp pain where you hit your head on some-thing hard.

Then...nothing.

Turn to page 44.

You and Hannah launch the canoe and paddle out of the cove. The wind blows violently, and whitecaps form at the top of each wave. This is going to be rough!

The rain pours down. You've never seen such a bad storm. The waves toss you about, and you are scared. A pool of water is forming in the bottom of your canoe. A big wave—then another—comes crashing into the boat. You're swamped!

Turn to the next page.

Just as you're about to give up, a huge figure dressed in flowing white robes appears out of the clouds. "I am a goddess, and this lake is my home. When I started this storm, I did not see you and your sister alone in your canoe. Do not worry. I will take you to shore myself."

With that, she scoops up your canoe in the palm of her hand and, smiling, deposits you safely at your dock. Before you can catch your breath to thank her, she disappears into the clouds, leaving a stream of brilliant pink light behind her.

The End

"It's getting too rough, Hannah! We have to go in now!"
You can barely hear your own voice over the wind, but
Hannah nods and begins to steer the canoe toward shore.
The wind is at your back. It helps to push you along. You
are almost there when the canoe hits a hidden rock.
Water comes gushing in through a hole in the bottom and
begins to fill the boat. Without another thought, you grab
your camera and jump into the lake.

Turn to the next page.

You'll have to swim the rest of the way. Hannah swims ahead and gets out first, helping you onto the slippery rocks. Just as you get a safe grip, Hannah says, "Look! can't believe it. Quick! GET A PICTURE!"

There, right where your canoe went down, is Champ playing in the storm. She dives in and out of the waves splashing you with her tail. You snap 24 pictures in all Wait until everyone sees these. It's a good thing you camera is waterproof!

The End

"Hannah, let's take the box back and open it with Grandpa's tools."

Hannah agrees, and the two of you walk back through the house. Just as you step off the porch, your sneaker lace gets caught and you trip. The box crashes into some rocks and breaks open. Inside there's an old green rag and an old jar of hand cream from the 1930s.

"Nothing but junk," Hannah says.

"Wait, Hannah. Look." You open the jar. Inside are four beautiful blue-green stones.

"They look like emeralds!" Hannah says excitedly. "Let's go back and show them to Grandpa and Grandma."

Turn to page 6.

You and Hannah run to the high rocks and scramble to the top. From here someone will see you. That is, if anyone is around.

You look for boats, but all you see are flashes of lightning. The rain is coming down hard and fast. You can't see very far. Will anybody notice you after all?

Just then you spy a boat about a half mile off. You and Hannah jump up and down, waving your arms and yelling. It seems to be turning toward you, but you can't be sure.

As the boat gets closer, you can see two people wearing uniforms. It is a Lake Champlain patrol boat.

You are safe!

The End

You and Hannah decide to break the lock right away. Hannah runs to get a rock. She lifts it high in the air and brings it crashing down on the lock. The lock doesn't break, but the old dry wood crumbles easily. Inside the box is an old-fashioned jar of hand cream wrapped in a wrinkled green rag.

Hannah frowns. "There's nothing here. Let's go look for Champ."

If you tell Hannah to go ahead while you finish looking around upstairs, turn to page 36.

If you want to continue your search for Champ, turn to page 40.

You'd still like to look around, so you tell Hannah to go along and that you'll be out in a few minutes. After she leaves, you open the jar. Inside are four beautiful blue-green stones that look like emeralds. Maybe they are emeralds!

Turn to the next page.

Suddenly you hear Hannah yelling, "Champ! Champ! I see Champ!"

You run as fast as you can downstairs. Outside you catch a glimpse of Champ's long neck and head before he dips below the surface.

In all the excitement, you forget about the jewels until you're paddling home. You'll have to go back to get them tomorrow!

The End

"You're right, Hannah. It's getting late, and we stil haven't seen Champ."

You retrace your steps through the house. As you pass a window, you catch a glimpse of a small head, two feet above water, looking curiously at the house. It's Champ!

Go on to the next page.

When you get outside, Champ leans her head back and cries, "Yaaooooo! Yaaooooo," in a thin, high-pitched voice. Six more creatures of different sizes appear in the cove. They stare at you and Hannah for several moments. Then Champ makes another cry, and all seven disappear together, back under the surface of the water.

Turn to the next page.

In a few seconds, the lake is calm as if nothing had happened.

The End

You wake up on the shore. The storm has passed. The sun is peeking through the clouds. Hannah is lying next to you, and the canoe is nearby, wedged between two rocks.

You don't remember exactly what happened. After you hit your head, you felt as if you were in a dream. You were floating face down in the water and couldn't move. Then, out of nowhere, an enormous creature that looked like a cross between a dinosaur and a seal lifted you onto its back and swam to shore. It left you safely on the shore.

You turned to see the creature before it left. All you saw was a big head with large blinking eyes. Was it Champ? Or were you dreaming?

Hannah is awake now, too. Rubbing her eyes, she says, "You know, I think we were saved. Did you see something that looked like a huge seal bring you to shore too?"

A happy shiver races down your spine. Maybe you weren't dreaming after all!

The End

CREDITS

Illustrator Keith Newton began his art career in the theater as a set painter. Having talent and a strong desire to paint portraits, he moved to New York and studied fine art at the Art Students League. Keith has won numerous awards in art such as The Grumbacher Gold Medallion and Salmagundi Award for Pastel. He soon began illustrating and was hired by Walt Disney Feature Animation where he worked on such films as *Pocahontas* and *Mulan* as a background artist. Keith also designed color models for sculptures at Disney's Animal Kingdom and  has animated commercials for Euro Disney. Today, Keith Newton freelances from his home and teaches entertainment illustration at the College for Creative Studies in Detroit. He is married and has two daughters.

This book was brought to life by a great group of people:

Shannon Gilligan, Publisher
Gordon Troy, General Counsel
Melissa Bounty, Senior Editor
Stacey Boyd, Designer

Thanks to everyone involved!

ABOUT THE AUTHOR

Shannon Gilligan at the Teatro la Fenice Ball, Venice, Italy.

SHANNON GILLIGAN is a well-known creator of interactive narrative games for the computer. She has spoken about interactive narrative and game design at conferences in Japan, Europe and the United States. Gilligan got her start in this field by writing for the *Choose Your Own Adventure®* series in the 1980s. Her books and games have sold several million copies around the world. She graduated from Williams College in 1981 and lives in Warren, Vermont with her husband R. A. Montgomery and her extended family. In 2003 she formed Chooseco with two partners to re-launch *Choose Your Own Adventure. Fabulous Terrible: The Adventures of You,* a new series for teen girls, is her latest creative project.

**For games, activities and other fun stuff,
or to write to Shannon Gilligan,
visit us online at CYOA.com**

Original Fans Love Reading
Choose Your Own Adventure®!

The books let readers remix their own stories—and face the consequences. Kids race to discover lost civilizations, navigate black holes, and go in search of the Yeti, revamped for the 21st century!
Wired Magazine

I love CYOA—I missed CYOA! I've been keeping my fingers as bookmarks on pages 45, 16, 32, and 9 all these years, just to keep my options open.
Madeline, 20

Reading a CYOA book was more like playing a video game on my treasured Nintendo® system. I'm pretty sure the multiple plot twists of *The Lost Jewels of Nabooti* are forever stored in some part of my brain.
The Fort Worth Star Telegram

How I miss you, CYOA! I only have a small shelf left after my mom threw a bunch of you away in a yard sale—she never did understand.
Travis Rex, 26

I LOVE CYOA BOOKS! I have read them since I was a small child. I am so glad to hear they are going back into print! You have just made me the happiest person in the world!
Carey Walker, 27